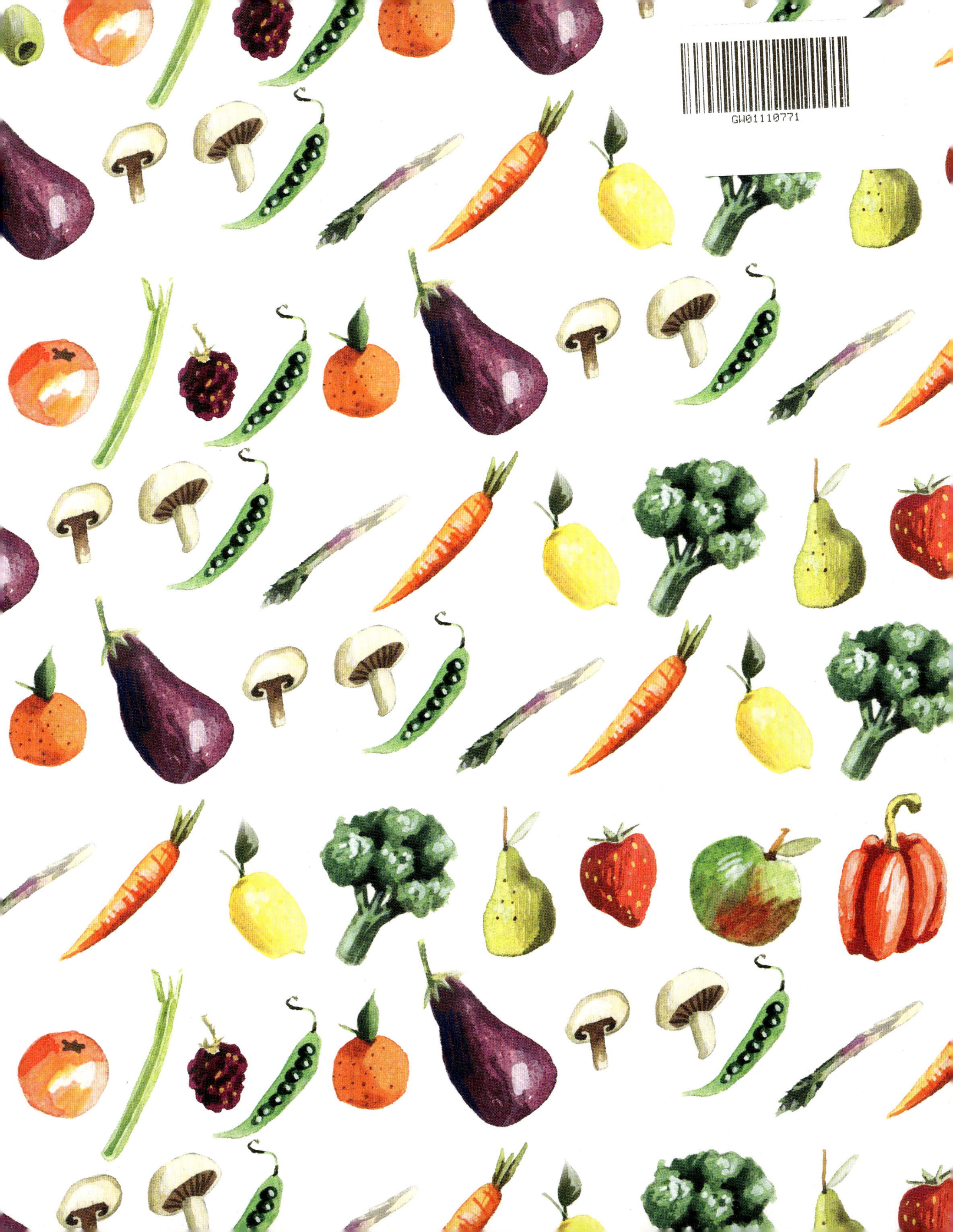

For my two little Supervegans
Lyla and Ada,
you inspire me every day.
This book is for you and the future generations.
Go and save the animals
and our planet with your vegan power! - TN

For Oshi & Oona - HCB

Text and illustrations copyright © Tina Newman 2019
Illustrations by Holly Clifton-Brown

All rights reserved. No part of this book may be reproduced or used in any manner without written permission of the copyright owner except for the use of quotations in a book review.

Printed and bound by L.E.G.O, September 2019, in Italy. L.E.G.O are partnered with FSC-certified printers using vegetable inks, recycled paper and 100% biodegradable laminates.

ISBN 978-1-9161036-0-3

Published by Tina Newman
www.vivithesupervegan.co.uk

Vivi the SUPERVEGAN

written by TINA NEWMAN

Illustrations by HOLLY CLIFTON-BROWN

Vivi Mirabelle looks just like you and me.

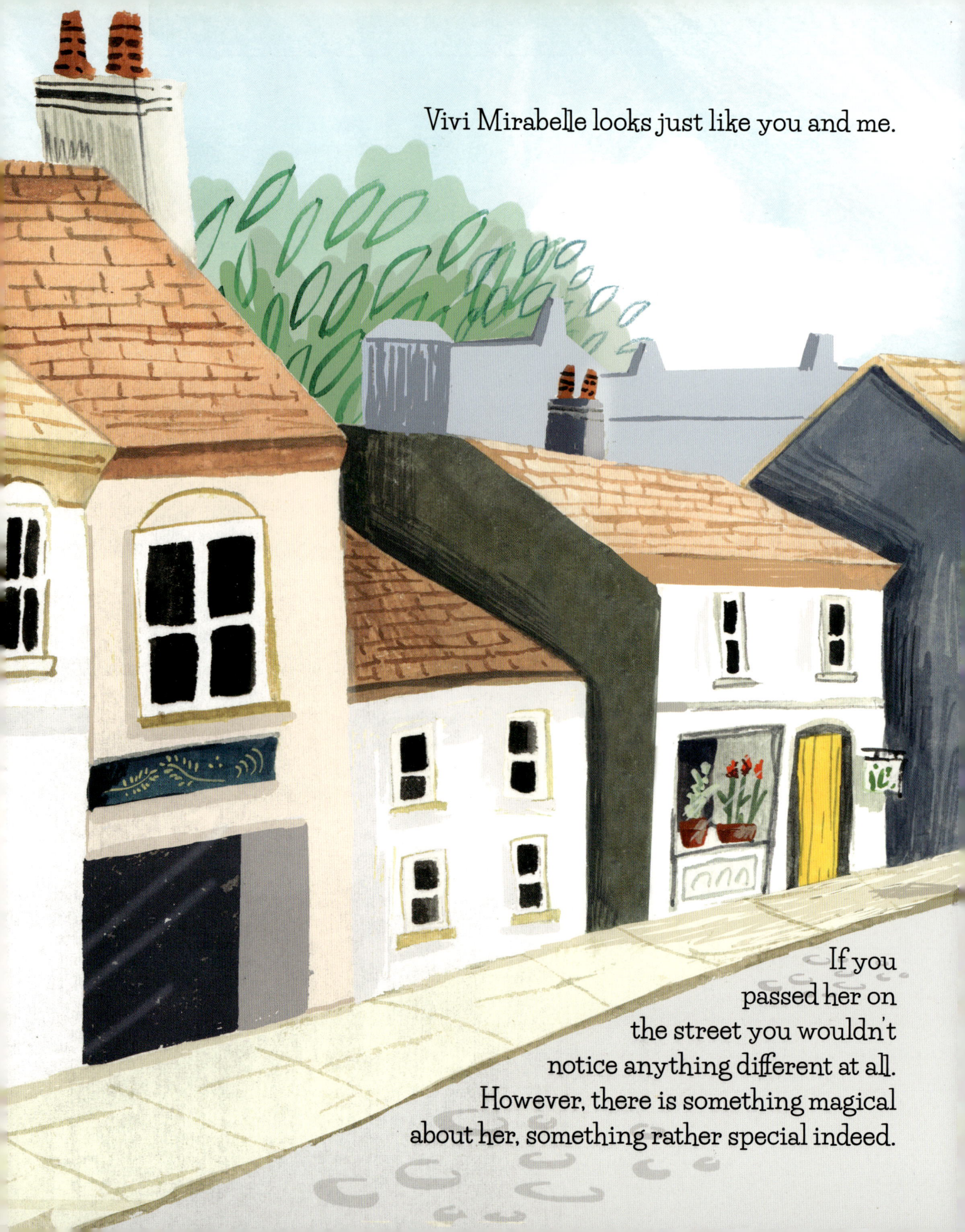

If you passed her on the street you wouldn't notice anything different at all. However, there is something magical about her, something rather special indeed.

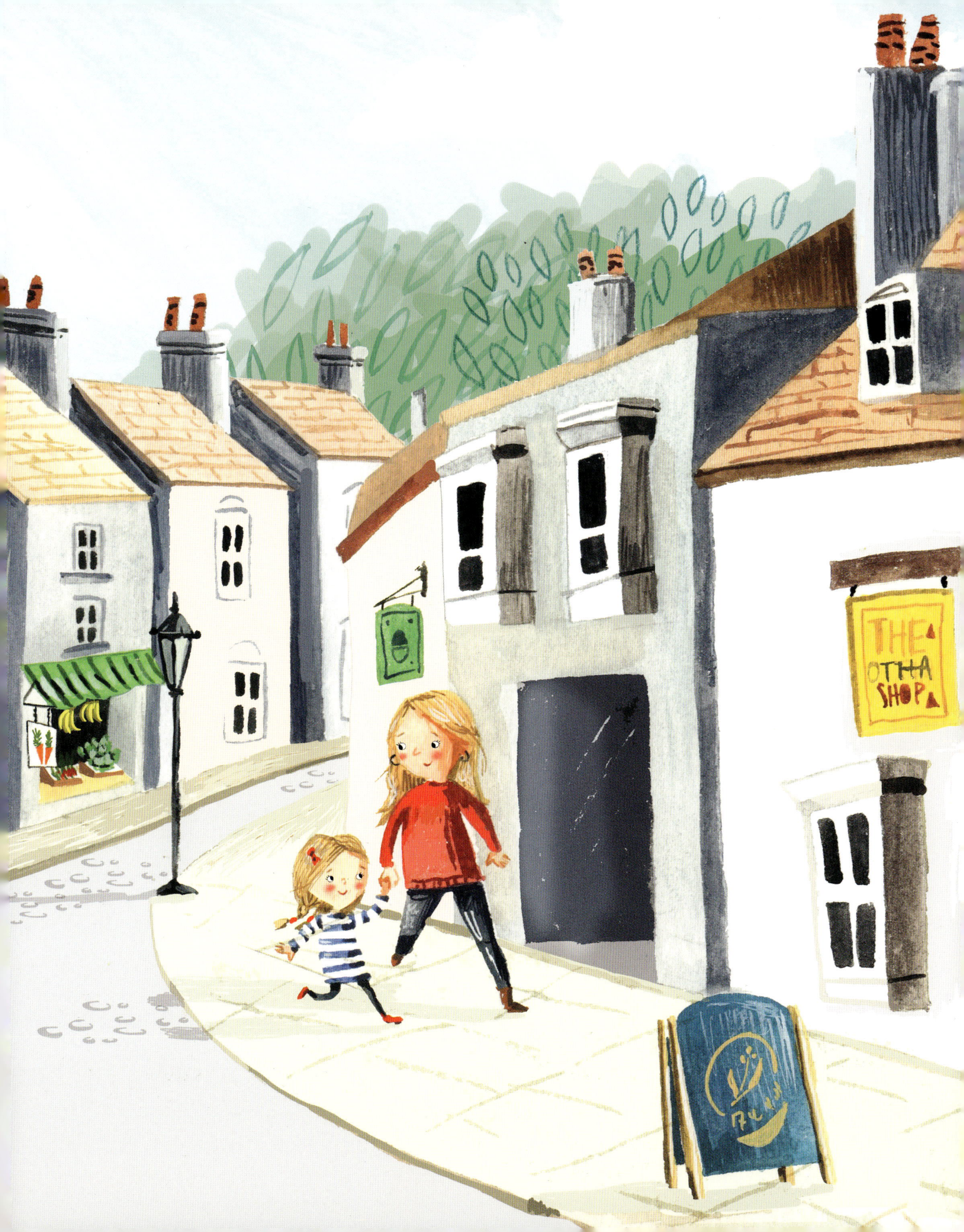
THE OTHA SHOP

You see, Vivi is a vegan.

She's powered by plants from her head to her toes,

using no animal products wherever she goes.

In fact, I'll let you in on a little secret...

Vivi is actually a
SUPERVEGAN

The first time she discovers she has magical powers is the day her parents rescue Fidget.

"Please help," the little chicken says, "humans are hurting us."

Vivi is so shocked that she can understand her, she nearly falls off her swing.

"We haven't done anything to them, why do they want to eat us?" Fidget says sadly.

Vivi's eyes start to sparkle as tears fall down her cheeks.

This always happens when she feels sad but she doesn't know why.

"I promise I will protect you and your friends and teach others to do the same," she says, stroking Fidget gently.

Since that day, every time Vivi twists her plait and taps her nose, she transforms into Vivi the Supervegan.

Being plant powered means that Vivi can do many amazing things and is gaining new powers all the time.

However, there are some that she can't control at all and one of those is called *Speculo*.

The first time this happens to Vivi is when she meets
Mrs Rufflefeather who lives next door. She is a
peculiar lady who smells of lavender and old slippers.

One day she pops over to visit Vivi's mother but when she sees Vivi she completely freezes on the spot. It is like she has turned into a statue, but she is crying and muttering something over and over again.

You see, *Speculo* happens when people look into Vivi's eyes.
She reflects the truth back at them and let's just say,
people don't always like what they see.

"How could I have been so blind to their suffering?" Mrs Rufflefeather whispers. "I'm never going to eat animals again!"

And from that day on, she doesn't.

One spring morning, Vivi's mother shares some exciting news.

"You're going to be a big sister," she beams, "Mummy is going to have a baby!"

Vivi is so excited she feels as though she may burst.

Some months later at school, Vivi is daydreaming when she suddenly notices a duck behaving rather strangely, trying to catch her attention. "Oh no," whispers Vivi. "She must need my help."

As soon as Miss Poppalot is distracted, Vivi makes a dash for the door.

"Where do you think you're going?" booms a voice from the corridor.

"Oh dinglebats!" mutters Vivi.

It is Mr Squigglesworth, the headteacher. He is peering over the top of his glasses and marching towards her like a dinosaur in welly boots.

Vivi knows she has to think quickly to distract him.

Spinning round and smiling sweetly, she gives a twist and a tap and suddenly Mr Squigglesworth is crawling around the floor behaving like a dog.

"Phew, that was close," giggles Vivi as she runs past, patting him on the head.

If you are worrying about him, you don't need to – he won't stay like that for long and he won't remember it either.

"Whatever's the matter?" Vivi asks as she reaches the frantic duck.

"You must come quickly!" he replies.

"A piglet has fallen from a truck and hurt his leg." With a twist, a tap and a flash of her cape they are gone.

When Vivi gets to the piglet he is scared and in pain. She carefully bundles him up in her cape and with another twist and a tap they are back in her bedroom.

"Oh, thank you so much," the tiny piglet says. "I am so frightened. I want my mummy and I don't know where she's gone."

Vivi lowers her head sadly, knowing where they would have taken her and where he had been heading on that truck.

"It is OK, you are safe now," she says, cuddling him tightly. Her eyes begin to sparkle and a single teardrop falls from her eye on to his leg.

"Wow... it doesn't hurt any more!" he squeals with delight. "How did you do that? Your eyes... they're sparkling so brightly."

It is at this moment that Vivi understands the reason for her magical eyes.

"I can't bring your family back but I promise to make sure you will live the rest of your life in peace and safety." With that she opens her window and whistles loudly.

There is a rustle in the bushes. "What's wrong?" says a huge horse, poking his head through the leaves.

"Hello, Reggie," says Vivi. "We must get our friend to the animal sanctuary PRONTO!"

Smiling at the piglet, Vivi asks him,
"What's your name?"

"I don't think I have one," he replies sadly. "They just used to call me 389."

"How about Button?" Vivi asks, tickling his tiny nose and wrapping him in a blanket.

The piglet smiles shyly and nods his head. "Button - I like that!"

Vivi tucks a small note under the blanket and lowers him on to Reggie's back.

"Go quickly and carefully, Reggie. Remember to wear your disguise so nobody spots you like last time!"

She waves goodbye to Button and with a twist and a tap she is back in her classroom.

"Vivi, will you please go to the office right away," says Miss Poppalot.

Oh no, Vivi thinks, *this time I must have been found out.*

She nervously scampers off to the office and is just about to give a twist and a tap to escape when she notices her father beaming from ear to ear.

"Vivi, Mummy is having the baby – we must go right away."

That evening, little Lily is born beneath the Christmas tree.

"Hello. I'm your big sister," says Vivi, cuddling her tightly. "We are going to have so many adventures together."

As Vivi passes her back to her mother she is sure she sees Lily tap her nose and give her a wink!

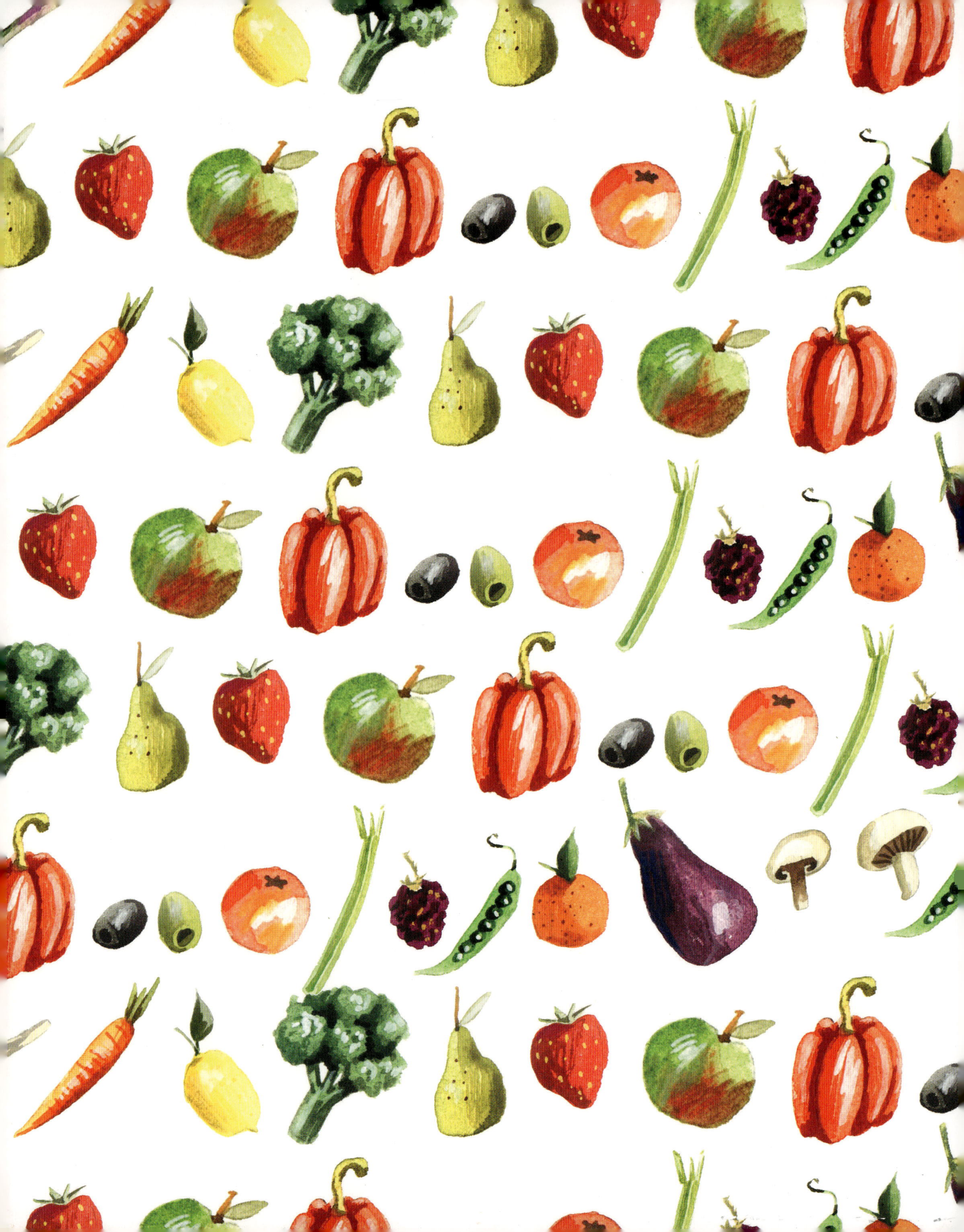